THE SHADOWS UNCOVERED

VEDANSHI CHIB

Contents

Preface

I grew up with a love of reading books, It was my dream to publish a book and here I am ready to publish one and making my dreams come true.

Sudha Murthy is the main inspiration for me to write this book, As a 12 year old I get really inspired by her. If she is reading this book (which is not likely) I would thank her profoundly for the inspiration that she gave.

This book is also inspired by my thoughts, so this book has been written to contribute my thoughts too.

Vedanshi Chib

Jammu ,

1

A Good Thought

Simhi was sitting on her bed playing with her toys when she suddenly heard the laughter of children outside, she went to a window which was opposite to her bedroom to see a beautiful site, children playing with their parents. While she was looking outside she noticed how happy those children were, her thoughts then suddenly shifted towards her parents, she realized that she knew nothing about them.

Now, with a determined look on her face, Simhi set off to find where MS Anny was. MS Anny was the caretaker of Simhi and other children who were in her dormitory, she was a tall women with a fair white skin with curly hair wearing glasses. She was a kind women who took care of all the children in the orphanage very well.

Simhi asked her in a serious tone, 'Mother, you have to tell me about my actual parents, how they died and how I ended up in this orphanage' MS Anny, who was a bit surprised by her sudden sternness, replied calmly, 'Child I have told you many times that your parents died because of an accidental fall from a high place in a factory'. Simhi who wasn't satisfied with her reply said in a questioning tone, 'But Mother, how come they died due to the fall? Didn't the people around them take any action? and moreover, where did my parents lived? What were there names? What.... 'I have no idea about this; you should just figure it out yourself;' ,interrupted MS Anny, who then went to another part of the dormitory to tackle other children.

Simhi had a lot of questions in her mind: why was MS Anny hesitant to reply? Why was she frustrated? But her thoughts got interrupted when the bell rang for dinner. Simhi had two friends; one was a girl whose name is Shynah, and the other was a boy whose name is Nand. Shynah was very shy in nature, she had come in this orphanage this year only, when her parents and her whole family were swept away by a cyclone and she was the only survivor due to this she was always in a depressed state, But after she became friends with Simhi and Nand her happiness was once again restored on the other hand Nand, who also had a similar story.

For eating, there was a very big dining hall where everyone sat to eat. The food was served in different varieties, and everyone gobbled it down, everyone except Simhi, who was deep in her thoughts and hardly ate or talked to anyone. Her friends had noticed her strange behavior and asked her for the reason, Simhi, who was in a very rare mood of expressing her feelings, blurted out everything about the conversation that she had with MS Anny.

Shynah laughed out loud after listening to her story. She did not take her seriously and she joked by saying, 'So, what would you do after that? MS Anny doesn't know about the information, so are you going to solve the mission or something?' But Nand was serious; he encouraged Simhi to solve this mystery.

Before Simhi could say something MS Anny came and escorted everyone to there bed as dinner time was over and it was there bed time, but Simhi could not fall asleep she was thinking about the happenings that happened in that day she recalled that MS Anny had told her after she questioned her about her parents " you should just figure it out yourself " and then she recalled Shynah saying "what would you do after that, MS Anny doesn't know about the information so are you going to solve the mission or something."

After recalling this she got encouraged to solve this mystery and to prove everyone wrong by solving it. The next day Shynah and Nand were waiting for Simhi to get ready for their morning walk but to there surprise Simhi who normally looked excited for morning walks refused to go, when Nand asked her the reason she simply said, 'I don't want to' and went to her bed.

Shynah decided to investigate and slowly opened the dormitory's door and went inside it, Shynah hid behind Simhi's bed, Simhi, who was very concentrated, did not realize it, Nand followed Shynah too. They heard Simhi mumbling something to herself. Nand suddenly sneezed, which made Simhi realize that they were hiding behind her bed.

'Why are you here?' asked Simhi in a demanding voice. 'W..we just wanted to see what you were doing' said Shynah, With a sigh Simhi pulled out her diary and turned to a page; that page contained various types of information that Shynah and Nand could not understand.

'What is this?' asked Nand, who was a bit confused. 'This is my plan for solving this mystery,' said Simhi. Simhi thought that her friends would laugh at her for doing this, but to her surprise Shynah chuckled and said in a soft tone,

'Simhi why are you solving this mystery on your own? What are we for?'

Simhi smiled and allowed them to sit with her on the bed and solve the mystery together.

'So here I have written the conversation that I had with MS Anny yesterday', said Simhi while showing her diary to Shynah and Nand.'Cool blueprint' exclaimed Nand but Shynah didn't say anything she was deep in her thoughts, 'What's the matter Shynah' continued Simhi 'Why aren't you saying anything? to which Shynah replied, 'I had seen in a ditective movie two years ago how to discover mysteries and it was some fascinating stuff maybe you can get some idea from there?'

Nand laughed, 'Movies are just a waste, they are not real'. Simhi listened to them for a while and decided to interrupt them, 'Maybe while we go to our morning walk we may come up with an idea.

2

A Crazy Shock

But before Simhi and her friends could discuss anything MS Anny came and told Nand, 'Nand, go to MS Madelline's office; she has called you urgently.'

This worried Nand and his friends because MS Madelline, who was the directress of the orphanage, did not like Simhi and her friends. She abutsed them. She even hated MS Anny. Although Simhi didn't really mind she still wanted to ask MS Madelline the reason for abutsing her so badly, butt she never asked, much to the relief of MS Anny.

Simhi also wanted to go with Nand, and she asked MS Anny if she could, butt she denied her request by saying, 'No, my child, MS Madelline has only asked Nand to go and no one else,' saying thus she went with Nand to escort him to the directress's office.

butt Simhi was curious. She had to investigate, so she told Shynah to stay in the dormitory and make some excuse to MS Anny about her going. She then went downstairs. She had never gone to the directress's office, there she saw many different rooms which she had never seen before.

There was another dormitory which may be for boys suspected Simhi as Nand always came from downstairs to wait for her and Shynah in the morning, then she discovered a hostel for the caregivers which was a few meters away from the boys dormitory, then on the left of her she saw different rooms made for different purposes and had labels on them like, there was a guest room, a donation room, a store room and much more. Simhi realized that her orphanage was bigger than she imagined.

She wandered a little further when she saw a room which had the label <u>The Directress Office,</u> this was what she was looking for, she had brought a paper and a pen along with her to note down any important stuff happening, she put her ear on the wall and started to note whatever she heard. Their were faint voices coming from the mistresses room, as the conversation between Nand and MS Madelline got deeper her stress too got higher.

After she listened a bit longer she left as she could not bear listening to their conversation any longer, Simhi who never cried suddenly felt her eyes stinging, she quickly rushed to her dormitory and threw the paper that she took with her on the astonished Shynah. Shynah rode the words on the paper aloud.

<u>MS Madelline</u> - *Dear we just got information that your uncle is alive, he will come tomorrow and take you to his home.*

<u>Nand</u> - *What!, I don't want to go I love this orphanage and want to stay here only.*

<u>MS Madelline</u> - *'Chuckled' I know you are joking.*

<u>Nand</u> - *butt....*

<u>MS Madelline</u> - *Ok now go to the guest room until your uncle MR. Rodger arrives to pick you.*

These words were scribbled on that piece of paper Shynah could see through how Simhi's handwriting changed from a beautiful cursive to a handwriting of a four year old that she was panicking. Shynah too became distressed butt still she tried to quite Simhi.

This was problematic for Simhi and Shynah because Nand's parents, who were very wealthy, when they died their wealth got transferred to there son, Nand gave money to MS Anny as a type of salary because MS Madelline hated MS Anny so much that she didn't even give her, her salary and neither allowed her to eat from the orphanage for free, the second reason for why they were worried was because of MS Madelline who hated Simhi and Shynah a lot, butt due to Nand which she knew was wealthy she did not abutsed Simhi and Shynah to a great extend as she feared Nand could take any action to oppose her.

butt the main reason for their sadness was because Nand was their best friend and all three of them were inseparable. Nand and Simhi's bonding felt inseparable.

'Can't Nand just deny to go as he has a very close bonding with us and especially with you' said Shynah thoughtfully, 'Yes he can butt the problem is that living with a family member and that to this rich and living a normal life is a very big dream for any orphan so most probably he would get tempted to go' said Simhi sadly.

They both then had dinner and went to sleep without Nand being a part of there fun.

Simhi couldn't sleep, she just toss and turned, she was thinking about Nand and the decision he would make then she couldn't take it any longer and jumped out from her bed, it was midnight at that time, the whole dormitory was filled with the soft snores of the children, Simhi crept to the little windoww there she saw a car coming towards the orphanage it was a luxurious car, 'It looks like it is a Mc Laren' thought Simhi then a man got out of a car, Simhi could barely see him properly as there was darkness outside he was a tall man wearing a long coat with long black boots and a big black hat with a golden feather on it, 'He looks like a spy' thought Simhi.

'This might be uncle Rodger, Nand's uncle' suspected Simhi, her suspicion was proven when MS Madelline greeted him and Nand ran to hug the man Simhi couldn't see clearly butt she felt the happiness and joy that Nand was feeling at that time.

Seeing Nand's happiness Simhi smiled to herself for the first time since morning, butt this happinesss lasted for a few seconds when Simhi suddenly realized that soon Nand would have to make the decision, Simhi heart started to beat loudly she had never been this stressed in her life.

She quickly wore her slippers and went downstairs, she wanted to meet Nand, it was a risky move butt Simhi didn't seem to bother. She knew where the Mistresses room was as she had gone there earlier she put her ear on to the wall of the mistresses office butt couldn't hear a thing, Simhi wondered what to do she then realized that there was a small windoww through which she peeked in, the window was closed but Simhi could see a little inside she saw the shadows of the furniture butt not of any human beings, so Simhi decided to butilt up some courage and do the unthinkable.

Simhi opened the Mistresses door, it was a risky move because if the Misstres was inside Simhi would have gotten into a big trouble, butt to her surprise no one was inside. Simhi switched on the lights and started investigating, there were many cabinets piled with books, it was an old fashion office it was a simple office with a chair, a desk, few couches and two bookshelves, it also had an old fashioned telephone in it.

While she was looking around she accidently hit herself with the table and an object fell on her foot she could not bear the sudden pain and screamed loudly.

Unfortunately MS Madelline heard it as there was noise of footsteps outside the mistress's office it sounded like more then one person coming inside the mistresses office, Simhi had to hide meanwhile MS Madelline rushed to her office with Nand and MR Rodger when she opened the door of her office she was alarmed.

Because she saw that the lights were on and her speciall keys were fallen down, 'Someone had entered my office' thought MS Madelline worriedly meanwhile Simhi had managed to hide under the desk really uncomfortably butt the problem was that if anyone would look straight down they would realize that she was hiding there, the only thing Simhi did at that time was praying to god and regretting to go to the mistress's office butt it was too late to change it.

MS Madelline who didn't want this incident to be shared with anybody just replied to Uncle Rodger nervously, 'Oh I maybe by mistakenly forgot to turn of the light'.

'Then what about the scream of a child MS Martha Madelline', asked Uncle Rodger a bit concerned, ' uh..h....uhhhhh' MS Madelline couldn't give a reply meanwhile Simhi who was listening to there conversation realized that Uncle Rodger was very concerned about the scream and would not let the matter slip out of his hands.

So she decided to take the matter in her own hands and started looking around where she saw a small pebble she took it and threw it towards them the pebble bounced from the wall and hit MS. Madelline.

Simhi was intending to hit MR Rodger not MS Madelline, MS Madelline who was hurt ran out of the room followed by Nand who also got scared and ran, 'Nand had told me many times that he is very brave butt now he got scared of a small pebble assuming it as a ghost' thought

Simhi who was not impressed.

Only Uncle Rodger who was wise did not followed them or got scared in fact he started to search from where the pebble cam from, ' I am done for' thought Simhi worriedly and that was what exactly had happened uncle Rodger found out where Simhi was hiding, 'who are you' asked Uncle Rodger sternly, ' I..I am Simhi sir' said Simhi meekly'.

'Why are you here' asked uncle Rodger Simhi didn't reply 'why are you here tell me otherwise I would call MS Martha Madelline' said uncle Rodger 'No sir please do not tell her I have come here because I cannot bear be apart from my friend Nand because he is one of my best friends' said Simhi with a deep sigh.

Uncle Rodger laughed he laughed and laughed madly, 'You are a brave girl Simhi so because of it Nand will not go anywhere butt he still has to go to school so he would come in the evening' said uncle Rodger, Simhi who was very happy thanked Uncle Rodger and went to her dormitory

3

An Unforgettable Discovery

The next day Simhi went straight towards Shynah and told her the whole 'adventure' that she had at midnight after listening to it, Shynah took a sigh of relief and said, 'now because of your adventure in the midnight, Nand does not have to go anywhere,' said Shynah excitedly.

But unfortunately Shynah spoke loudly because of it MS Anny who was nearby heard it, 'what were you two up to in the midnight? asked MS Anny,' 'we were not doing anything other than sleeping' replied Simhi, ' were you sleeping, or had you gone to MS Madelline's office and caused havoc?' asked MS Anny.

'But how can you know Mom?' asked Simhi, a bit surprised. 'MS Madelline has told me about it and she is expecting you to do it as she knows how much mischief you create and that she' continued MS Anny 'never misbehave again like that without my permission otherwise you and I would be in a serious trouble', Simhi promised not to do it again.

Nand entered their conversation by saying, 'without Simhi, I would not be here right now.' Simhi and Shynah were happy to see Nand staying with them MS Anny was also surprised to see Nand, 'Why had MS Madelline called you?' Nand just smiled and said it was for a small reason and Nand with his friends left the shocked MS Anny behind and went to play together.

While Simhi was playing with her friends, she recalled yesterday's adventure. While she was thinking about it, she remembered an object falling on her foot she asked Nand, 'Why did MS Madelline said that her secret keys had fallen yesterday' Nand replied casually, ' Oh, that was the key for her library'.

'But the library doesn't have a door because it is attached to MS Madelline's office' said Simhi, Nand suddenly realized that Simhi was right, and there was no door for the library Nand also started to think curiously about the reason for MS Madelline saying it to be a library's key.

Simhi now wanted to investigate more, so she told Nand and Shynah to continue playing. Simhi went to the mistress's office she knew that MS Madelline was not at her office because she had to attend a meeting, which gave Simhi plenty of time to investigate.

Simhi entered the mistress's office, this time she was not stressed unlike the last time so she had more time to look around the office. It was a small office which had walls painted in a burnt brown color the decor was in an old fashion style she looked around and noticed an opening which led to a small library, she saw a key on the desk of the office now Simhi recalled that it was the same key which had fallen on her foot that day she took the key and went into the library, the library had a small collection of old fashion books as Simhi was looking around she slipped and fell down while she slipped her hand flung on a book in a book shelf she then felt it being pressed down when she looked at it she saw a keyhole.

She then realized that the key she was holding in her hands was the perfect fit for the key hole when she unlocked it, she saw something that made her spine shiver.

A very big room which was in a very bad condition with cobwebs here and there. Simhi was scared to investigate herself so she locked the door kept it back in the mistress's office and went to the dormitory.

When her friends saw her they got excited, 'Have you discovered something?' shouted Nand. Which almost made the girls fall, 'Yes, I found a secret room behind the library, but I was too scared to investigate myself. 'Let's go together,' said Simhi but Shynah was scared, 'What if there are monsters their? Nand replied, 'Then I am going to kill it.' After listening to this, Simhi laughed and said, 'The person who gets frightened by a mere pebble thrown beside him, how could someone like him fight a mighty ghost?' she intended to embarrass Nand, Shynah laughed after listening to this and they all went to the mistress's office.

Then, when they entered the room Simhi turned on the flashlight to see many wooden crates. They were their for a while because it was covered with dust and cobwebs when Simhi opened one of the crates with great difficulty, and when it finally opened, she saw different dresses of a women and a man and of a child it all seemed strange but familiar to Simhi then she was about to open the second crate when Shynah screamed, 'MS Madelline is coming into the office', Shynah who was too scared to go in that room so she became the watch person to alert if anyone is coming.

Simhi quickly rushed along with Nand out of the office with Shynah but while they were going MS Madelline saw them but thankfully she didn't see their faces, 'come here you three why have you entered the office' asked MS Madelline with a strict tone the children stopped, 'don't look at MS Madelline otherwise she would know that it is us and plus she doesn't like us she will surely punish us so the best thing is to run' and that was exactly what they did this, 'stop right there' yelled MS Madelline but the children didn't listened and kept running until they reached their dormitory Nand said goodbye to them and went to his dormitory whereas Simhi and Shynah went to theirs.

while they were discussing about the mysterious adventure MS Anny interrupted them by saying, 'Children MS Madelline has appointed two hefty guards outside the girls and boys dormitory for some reason are you two responsible for this because I think you are'

'no we have done nothing wrong mom' they both said at once.

The next day in the early hours of the morning there was a knock on the door Simhi who just woke opened it thinking it was Nand but to her surprise it was uncle Rodger, 'hello what was your name again sSi... sim..simhs no simha no simhi yes Simhi where is Nand he has to go to school today is his first day' said uncle Rodger Simhi said that Nand was in the dormitory downstairs but as uncle Rodger was leaving Simhi called him, 'uncle Rodger.... I have something to tell you something secret I am telling you this because I feel you to be wise enough to talk to' said Simhi a bit hesitently' , 'speak out'said uncle Rodger.

so Simhi told the whole adventure she had in the library and said, 'uncle Rodger could you please report it to the police it seems scary for me to uncover this I think MS Madelline has some wrong intensions' uncle Rodger laughed and said, 'you are brave little one and it is good my nephew has made you as his friend but we do not have enough evidence do a bit more searching and the n I would report it to the police little detective' Simhi thanked uncle Rodger, 'and' continued uncle Rodger 'call me only uncle I have searched the meaning of your name it is lioness so I would call you little lioness from now onwards, your parents have given a fitted name to you' saying this he went to find Nand.

Simhi felt relief that some grownup finally understood him he was the first grown up to encourage Simhi to keep doing her investigation Simhi had first time been praised by someone now she got even more motivation than before to solve her mysteries.

4
An Break Through Escape

When MS. Anny asked Simhi who was sitting on her bed playing, 'Who was on the door? and why were you smiling?' Simhi replied 'Uncle Rodger was at the door but mom you won't understand why I was smiling but I just thell you this thing that I got a new best friend - or you can say I got a new family member'.

MS Anny was puzzled by Simhi's talkings, 'What do you mean?' asked MS Anny. 'You won't understand mom' saying thus Simhi went to find Shynah leaving the puzzled MS Anny all by herself.

Shynah was talking to Sina at a corner. Simhi came and asked them about their discussions. Sina replied, 'Oh, I was talking to Shynah about how MS. Madellinee is very strict with the children. Now she has hired guards to guard both the girls' dormitory and the boys' dormitory. No child is allowed to go to go to the different dormitories, so you cannot meet your Nand at any time soon'.

Simhi froze for a second, then she thanked Sina for the information and took Shynah with her to her bed.

'What about the plan how will we encover the mystheries? continued Simhi 'And moreover who appoints guards inside the dormitories, this is a lack of privacy'

Shynah replied, their are guards outside so how can we go out we have to stay we can't do anything about it...' Simhi intheruppthed, 'Shynah, what are you talking about?, nothing is impossible you should just have fathe in it and it will become possible'

'So are you saying that you have a plan to get to the library' asked Shynah in disbelieve, 'Yes, you are complethely right' said Simhi with a grin on her face.

'Here is the plan' said Simhi who then whispered something in Shynah's ear, 'Let's not discuss anything about this anymore and wait for midnight to complethe the plan other's would be suspecious if we talk the whole day about this only and don't act normally and I *ought* to have a break from this conversation even' So, Simhi and Shynah starthed to play and acthed complethely normal.

They played all kinds of games and then it was time for dinner then they went in the dinning hall there everyone was seathed and clear whithe plathes were already there the only thing left was to eat, few minuthes lather the meal was brought and the whole table were filled with hungry children who kept eying the food. It was a mixture of various things there were different varieties of *dall* and also there were chapatis and rice too along with orange juice and curd afther all this thea was served with toast and a few biscuits it was a scrumptious meal and ever one enjoyed it.

Afther Dinner the children had one hour for themselves before their bed time Sina wondered why Simhi wasn't feeling sorrowful for Nand as she cannot meet him. Sina always envies Simhi because everyone loves her and want to make friends with her insthead of Sina. So, she went to

Simhi and asked, 'What's the matther why aren't you sad that you can't meet your *friend* Nand anymore?, Isn't he your *best* friend or something'.

Simhi replied, 'Oh I have a plan up on my sleeves I know I am going to meet Nand and discuss really important matthers with him and how? well I got a plan up on my sleaves so you needn't to worry about it'. Shynah was listhening quithely at the corner and starthed to suspect that something is fishy with Sina as she knew how kind Sina was but now she is acting oddly. So before the argument got further Shynah pulled Simhi back and told her to stop, 'Something is fishy Simhi I think Sina doesn't like you as she never acts in this way with anybody'.

'You are right I have to control myself plus I have to save up my energy for today's midnight too', said Simhi, no sooner did she say these words the bell rang for bedtime, 'What a coincidence' exclaimed Shynah.

When the day ended and midnight struck Simhi's mind starthed to go crazy with the plans. She went towards Shynah's bed, Shynah who was just prethending to sleep when saw Simhi knew that it was time to executhe their plan. Simhi took her bedsheet cover and took Shynah's tied it together, then they both also tied the pillow covers of their beds. Afther tying all of those together their escape plan was ready, then Shynah threw the newly made rope out of the window and pressed it hard on to the wall and then Simhi climbed down from the building.

But their was a problem, the rope was not that long enough to touch the ground, it was a few inches short, so Simhi asked Shynah to throw the pillows at her, when Shynah did. Simhi threw it to the ground, then she loosen the grip of her fingers and let herself fall on to the ground due to the soft cushioning below Simhi didn't get hurt, then

Simhi threw the pillows back at Shynah and said her to untie the rope and keep it on the bed.

Simhi then gone a bit further ahead when she saw MS Madellinee there with a torch light, 'She seems to be searching for something' said Simhi to herself, Simhi didn't want to take any risk and hid behind a bush very uncomfortably.

Meanwhile Shynah had kept everything in a very proper way but before Shynah could heave a sigh of relief she heard footstheps Shynah panicked she quickly kept a pillow under the bedsheet of Simhi's bed in such a way that it looked like an actual person was sleeping then she quickly went to sleep.

The footstheps came nearer and nearer and it turned out to be MS Anny, 'So Sina was saying Simhi could be up to something let me check her bedroom', she said to herself softly. Shynah's heartbeat got fasther and fasther she couldn't believe that Sina had told MS Madellinee this, MS Anny came near to Simhi's bedroom, 'What's this Simhi is sleeping I must keep an eye on this girl if she hasn't done anything now then she would do something in the morning' said MS Anny to herself.

MS Anny was about to leave when she thought, 'Let me check if she *really* is in her bedroom sleeping' so saying thus she came near to Simhi's bedroom, 'I have to do something' thought Shynah.

MS Anny was coming nearer to Simhi's bed she was about to remove the blanket when Shynah thinking quickly took her hair pin which was kept at her shelf and threw it near MS Anny, then she took another hair pin and threw it near the dormitories door. MS Anny was startled, she quickly got up to follow the noise.

Shynah heaved a sigh of relief and thought, 'This time I have saved Simhi's plan from failing by luck but I have to be careful Sina can do *anything* '.

Meanwhile MS Madellinee while searching outside the orphanage had a book in her hand which she held very tightly, she took out her key from her pocket which looked like the same key of the library and opened what seemed like a trap door, then she went inside it.

Simhi couldn't understand, it all seemed exciting for her she was confused what to do, she thought that she would solve it with the help of her friends so she went to the entrance of the orphanage and headed straight towards the boys dormitory. But, there was a problem, there were guards infront of the boy's dormitory. Simhi thought hard but could not find any solution her mind was wandering thinking about MS Madellinee and the unusual trap door which she had never seen.

She then saw a stick that lay nearby, she threw the stick in the opposithe direction to distract the guards which worked, while they were distracthed Simhi went inside the boy's dormitory there were many beds in the dormitory and there were darkness everywhere so Simhi can't see properly Simhi had to think of something quickly because the guards would come again.

So Simhi quickly thought something, 'I have to take the risk otherwise I would be in trouble'. Simhi felt around the walls to find the light switch, she was inthending to turn on the lights, 'If any boy is waken up due to this I am in serious trouble' thought Simhi. She took a deep breath and turned on the light switch, nobody woke up. Taking a sigh of relief Simhi went to find Nand it was much easier to find him as there was a source of light. She saw Nand afther a while of looking he was sleeping in his night dress, 'wake up' whispered Simhi.

Nand woke up he was startled to see Simhi, 'What are you doing here' continued Nand, 'it doesn't matther you had came hear to meet me or anything but *how* in the world have you come hear....' But before Nand could say anything a boy had awoken up, 'Hurry do something' so Simhi quickly switched off the lights and was inthending to leave the room when it suddenly clicked in her mind that there were guards outside! Simhi was stuck she went to Nand and asked him for help.

'Quickly hide under my blanket' saying so Simhi did. The boy had woken up he had got up to go to the bathroom. Simhi was still as a stone she was afraid she would have been caught, she hid there for about five minuthes when the boy came back and slept.

'That was a close call you can come out of my blanket now' said Nand 'thank god you hid because that boy whose name is Ronald is really a type of theacher's pet if he had seen you he *ought* to have made a tantrum.'

Simhi told Nand everything and told him about the plan too, she told him to follow her, so off they went Simhi distracthed the guards again this time throwing pebbles to distract them.

They both went upstairs and distracthed the guards infront of the girl's dormitory in the same way and opened the door to get Shynah who was waiting inside, the trio then went outside and hid behind a bush, 'I saw MS Madellinee going from this side' continued Simhi 'Let's see were does this lead to'.

Simhi and her friends went near the bush in which MS Madellinee had disappeared, Simhi switched on the torch when she saw a trap door which was very hard to see as it was disguised. Simhi tried to open the door but it was locked.

Nand and Shynah too tried to open the trap door but to their avail they couldn't. Afther thinking what to do a sudden sound came from beneath the trap door. 'It must be MS Madelline she is coming here run' cried Simhi.

Simhi was right MS. Madellinee had came out of the trapdoor, all the three children ran and hid behind a bush when they felt the coast was clear they came out, 'it is too risky right now I think the best thing to do is to go back to our dormitories' said Shynah, the other two agreed, 'tomorrow is Sunday so Nand you can spend some time tomorrow so we would decide everything tomorrow' said Simhi.The three girls went back to their dormitories quietly and somehow managed to distract the guards again.

While they were back in their dormitories Shynah told everything to Simhi that happened afther she had gone, 'Sina has betrayed us she is jalouse of you.'

'I will see to it' said Simhi who was already tired and in no mood to discuss about this topic.

5
Solving Unsolved Mysteries

The next day Simhi got cramps most probably because of the yesterday's adventure, though it was normal for Simhi MS Anny panicked she started asking questions to Simhi about yesterday's events Simhi who was unable to bear the burden and almost told her about the whole adventure that happened yesterday when Nand inturrupted, 'Mam it's time for breakfast the bell rang'. Everyone was surprised to see Nand, 'Nand aren't you supposed to be in your dormitory how did you escape the guards' asked MS Anny.

'Mam the guards had left the door fifteen minutes before the break begun so I used this chance to escape' said Nand with a grin on his face. The three went to the dinning hall and sat there to have their meal, it was a lovely meal of a mixture of a deep fried bread made from whole wheat flour and a type of chickpea curry known as *poori* and *channa*. It was a scrumptious meal which delighted the students who ate it.After the meal the three started to discuss about the yesterday's events as there was a little time left before the bell rang.

'What could have MS Madelline be doing inside that trap door' continued Simhi 'we ought to find out' everyone agreed to investigate it further, 'I think we should first search the library again because it may hold some secrets' said Nand, the other two agreed, but before they could say anything further the bell rang and they had to go to their dormitories.

The day went by without much happening and at night Shynah who was preparing to sleep when MS Anny asked her where Simhi was, 'Oh she must be in the washroom washing her face and changing into her night dress' said Simhi casually and went back to prepare her bed for sleep.

When Simhi came out of the washroom MS Anny asked her to come with her to a corner of the room where no one would be able to hear them, Simhi was concerned after seeing the look in MS Anny's face.

'Listen up young girl MS Madelline is blaming you to do some mischief' continued MS Anny 'I know you haven't because how can you, but anyway I am keeping you as an discipline in charge for tomorrow your job is to discipline the room as I would not be here for an hour because I got an emergency.'Simhi replied, 'yes I could do it for you'.

The next day Simhi as soon as she woke up told Shynah what had happened yesterday Shynah suspected that MS Madelline was the cause of MS Anny's sudden going but anyways Simhi kept her promise and took care of the other children well.

An hour passed Simhi looked at the clock no sign of MS Anny... another hour passed STILL no sign of MS Anny this went till evening when Simhi couldn't take it any longer-WHERE *was* MS Anny.

Nand had finished his school work with the help of Uncle Rodger and had just returned to his room from his study area and Uncle Rodger had already fed Nand snacks so he didn't come to the snack break but Simhi and Shynah who were their got a plan to investigate where MS Anny was they went and ate their snacks quickly and ran to the principal's office where their was no one.

The two saw the key to the secret bookshelf door and took it with them to the library where they opened the door and went in there they saw the usual dark place with cobwebs everywhere, while they were searching they heard footsteps from outside after which Simhi quickly shut the door but forgot to lock it, she went to hide behind a bookshelf followed by Shynah who too hid behind another bookshelf.

There they could here the conversation between two people, there the two voices sounded much like the voices of MS Madelline and MS Anny, 'It sounded like MS Madelline was scolding MS Anny about something' thought Simhi, but she couldn't hear it clearly so she couldn't make out what they were saying.

They argued for a little time and then everything became quite, Shynah was getting impatient she couldn't stand much longer, a little while later there were again sounds of footsteps but this time it sounded like they were leaving the room.

6

Trapped In The Dungeons

They waited for a little while to see if any more sounds could be heard but there wasn't anymore so Simhi who was already enraged because of her mom getting scolded could not contain herself and went out of her hiding spot to go back to the library but to her utter shock MS Madelline was there sitting on her desk, it was evening that time, and Simhi couldn't do anything as neither Nand was there nor was MS Anny, Simhi stood there still to her utter horror when she saw Shynah too coming out of her hiding spot.

'What are you doing young ladies come here' said MS Madelline. Shynah and Simhi didn't respond to her, MS Madelline continued 'Why *are* you here reply me........ I said *reply ME*'

The only word that Simhi could utter at that momeant was to call for MS Anny, MS Anny who was always with her side, always comforted her when she felt scared but alas there is no MS Anny anywhere to be seen.' Oh so you are MS. Anny's children I see that *fool* hasn't taught you anything look - you two are coming with *me* because you know a lot about me and my plans but before anything happens you are at the end my children so wait here I just give you both some water, here you go' Simhi felt odd at her sudden change of behavior but still accepted the water Shynah with her shacky hands grasped on to the water cup when suddenly MS Madelline punched her on her head which made her faint. Simhi was horrified to see this and also fainted because of the shock.

When Simhi opened her eyes she found herself sleeping on a rock! Simhi was shocked, she got up and stood properly only to realized that she has been locked up in a type of cave, it felt like a prison sell, Simhi quickly tried to wake up Shynah, Shynah's head was hurting badly most probably because of MS. Madelline beating her up badly but still she managed to wake up.

'What should we do we are trapped' asked Simhi, 'That wretch Madelline is obviously behind all this' replied Shynah. 'Look water is leaking from above which means we are under ground I have read in a book that if you are confused that you are underground or above you can just check if any water is leaking anywhere this would mean there is a puddle of water above.' exclaimed Simhi, they were right Simhi and Shynah were actually underground.

' Do you have any escape plan, have you read *that* in any of your books because that is important right now' asked Shynah. They both were terified of the cave, who would have thought they would end up like that!

'No I havn't read any thing like that in any of my books sadly, thought I would thing of an escape plan.'

Both of them were thinking of an escape plan but could not seem to figure out any plan, they both thought hard but nothing entered in their mind.

'I say' continued Simhi, 'Let's explore this place, see for some clues or something'

The place really looked like a cave of some sort, it didn't have much to explore, there was a small torch light hooked to the wall and there were two big rocks and few smaller rocks here and there.

'Do you hear that?' asked Shynah 'sounds of footsteps! who would *ought* to wander here at such a scary place.'

'It must be that Madelline' replied Simhi with a frown on her face. They heard the footsteps coming nearer and nearer towards them. The footsteps coming near them were of MS Madelline!

'Hi children I hope you like your new home here you go - some food and water' said MS Madelline and gave the girls two tin which were suspiciously light thus she handed the food and water over and went back.

Simhi remembered the fun times at her orphanage, how she played with the others and how much fun she had. She cursed herself for trying to solve this mystery about finding her parents and about her 'secret mission'.

Simhi then felt her pocket and realized that she still had the library key though it was useless now Simhi still thought to keep it with her.

'What should we do now MS. Madelline has left us here all alone' continued Shynah, 'Do you thing that we are trapped here for ever!'

'Shut up! Shynah you ought not to scare me more, let me think of a plan' but she couldn't, 'Let's eat because I am really hungry and maybe I will think of a plan afterwards' said Simhi.

But when the girls took out the old dusty cloth which was covering their food they were shocked and horrified at the same time ; the food contained one dry chapatti for each with a little curd.

'How are we supposed to eat that' exclaimed Shynah, 'It feels inedible to me, even the chapatti is only one and there is not even *ghee* applied on it and who in the world will eat only *one* I am starving this is a real torture.'

The both girls ate the food not willingly even though it felt and looked almost inedible, Simhi had never seen such a thing in her life, she was so used to in eating delicious meals in the orphanage and could not simply imagine what kind of food this is.'

'Let's go to bed.. I meant sleep on some comfy place as their is no bed over here' said Shynah. So the two children slept really uncomfortably on the two big rock and took the two dusty sheets that were used as covers for covering their food that MS Madelline had given to them as blankets.

'Uh... the blanket is literally the width of my hand how are we supposed to sleep with *that* it is freezing out here' wailed Shynah

7

A Wonder For Nand

Meanwhile Nand after resting for a while in the evening woke up, he thought of Simhi and Shynah he waited for Dinner to talk to them. After impatiently waiting for the bell to ring it finally rang.

Nand went rushing towards the Dinning hall just to find Simhi and Shynah missing. Nand became worried he asked MS Anny about were they were to which MS Anny replied', 'What do you mean by Simhi and Shynah I thought they were coming with you'. 'But I haven't seen them' said Nand.

'They must be in MS Madellinee office then' said MS Anny worriedly. The whole day went silently both MS Anny and Nand were waiting for Simhi and Shynah to come , but obviously they didn't arrive because they were trapped in the dungeons.

The next day the guards also disappeared from outside the dormitories still MS Anny couldn't figure out why Simhi and Shynah hadn't come till now. MS Anny suspected Simhi to do some mischief which MS Madellinee may have caught and did something horrible to them to punish them and ironically the guards too disappeared unknowingly just a day after Simhi and Shynah dissapeared, MS. Anny knew

Simhi very well, she new what kind of mischiefs she does and MS Anny also knew that Simhi would do anything to know more about her parents.

Nand was very much relieved from the disappearing of the guards as this meant he could talk to MS Anny and ask her about Simhi and Shynah, so he didn't waste a single moment and went straight to the dormitory upstairs. 'Has Simhi and Shynah arrived?' asked Nand who almost made MS Anny fall, 'No dear sadly they haven't arrived till now' replied MS Anny. Nand was horrified, what had happened to Simhi and Shynah.

Nand didn't waste a single second and went to the mistress's office to ask about the two girls. MS. Madellinee was surprised to see Nand theree, 'Oh what happened dear you look very angry what's the matter and why haven't you went to school you should have been theree right now'. Nand payed no interest in her talkings he straight forwardly asked, 'Where have you kept Simhi and Shynah you wretched women' hearing this made MS. Madellinee extremely angry but she calmed down because she knew that if she would say something then Nand's uncle would not be very happy.

She burst into laughters and her tone changed from a kind voice to a high pitched annoying one which made Nand jump, 'You want to see them young man but it would be impossible because those two are adopted, somebody adopted both of them' she lied, Nand now speechless went to meet MS Anny and almost in tears blurted out everything to her.

The horrified MS Anny knew that it was all a lie she knew that for an adoption to take place there are many steps involved and the caretaker is also informed about it but she was horrified to think about what *had* happened to Simhi and Shynah, 'They must have been trapped somewhere' thought MS Anny.

Wasting no time MS Anny told Nand to play with the otheres and she went herself to MS Madelline's office and quit. MS Madellinee was pleased, 'Well if you say so'.MS Anny did all the formalities and quit her job.

Nand had realized that MS Anny had quit when he saw a new care taker getting appointed in the girl's dormitory where Simhi and Shynah were in, he knew that it was time for him to tell it to Uncle Rodger the next day while uncle Rodger was waiting outside early in the morning waiting to pick Nand up. Nand told everything to Uncle Roger who was surprised though he didn't believe on what Nand was saying much to Nand's disappointment he knew that something was off about MS Madellinee.

On the othere hand Simhi and Shynah didn't found any way to escape from the dungeons Shynah's was recovering slowly, many days passed MS Madellinee gave them food in the morning and noon Shynah thought that it was it, they are stuck this way for theree life time but Simhi didn't give up hope.

8

Prisoners

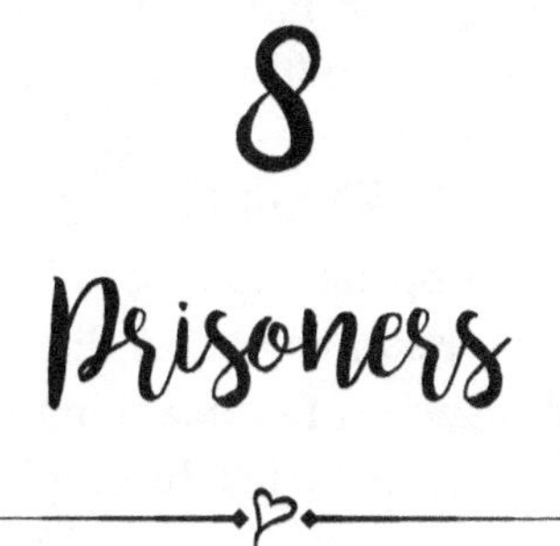

After three days of being stuck in the dungeon Simhi and Shynah grew very weak they lost all there hopes, it was evening at that time Simhi and Shynah hadn't seen the sun for three days they got disconnected with the outer world, they didn't knew the time and neither they were interested to know.

MS Madelline had just now given Simhi and Shynah their lunch, 'Here eat this or die' said MS. Madelline roughly then the same thing happened as always MS. Madelline gave them food and water and locked the door and went. While Simhi and Shynah were eating there not so appetizing food they heard a noise outside they suspected that they were just hallucinating but the voice got closer and closer 'tick' came a sound outside, 'Who is it' asked Simhi suspecting it to be MS Madelline but to the both Shynah and Simhi's surprise it was MS Anny! Simhi burst into tears and ran hugging MS Anny like a child would do after seeing her mother for a long time, MS Anny felt sorry for Simhi and especially sorry for Shynah who had a very big bruise on her head.

MS Anny didn't waste a single moment and just said, 'children I have to go you navigate through the dungeon yourself I know you can do it' and after saying this she ran away.

Simhi was puzzled and sad but she was thankful that at least the door was opened both Simhi and Shynah went outside there little prison to realize that they were not in a cave but in a dungeon it felt like a maize but still Simhi got some courage and took her flashlight which she had and packed some food and went to another adventure along with Shynah.

Fifteen minutes passed Simhi and Shynah were walking tirelessly while they were going they found themselves stuck and confused because they were surrounded by different entrances but Simhi noticed a faded light in two of the holes so Simhi decided to follow one of them if one goes to a dead end then the other would surely be the escape route.

So Simhi and Shynah went on there journey they took one tunnel with a faded light at the end and then began to walk again then they realized that the faded away light was actually a torch light put obviously by a person Shynah was relieved to see this because this meant that MS Madelline had went here so it is safe.

While Simhi and Shynah were walking a bit further the narrow path became wider and wider and taller and teller when at one point it reached at least two stories in height Simhi realized that they were very deep underground.

The dungeon felt unending Shynah suddenly started to feel hungry so they both decided to eat their food so they sat down on the rough surface to eat after they finished Shynah who was still very injured didn't had enough energy to walk any further so they decided to walk a bit further to find some soft place to sleep.

Shynah sat there and snoozed of to sleep on the rough floor Simhi smiled and sat beside her Simhi too dozed off.

When they woke up next day they continued their journey they went on and on when they finally reached there destination it was a very long journey but finally they reached the end of the path there were unusual surprises there was different crates scattered around it was a shocking discovery for Simhi, when Simhi and Shynah opened one of the crates they saw a child's dresses it looked about two years, they opened more and more crates.

In one of them there were dress's of a man and in another there were dress's of a women, Simhi couldn't understand a thing she told Shynah to look for more crates while they were searching Simhi found a pendulum where it was written *my little lioness.*

Simhi was confused and wondered why MS Madelline had these stuff while Simhi was wondering about it Shynah exclaimed Simhi there's a family photo here, she showed Simhi, 'but what does it all mean' exclaimed Simhi.

Shynah was desperate to escape said, 'Let's go we would later investigate I do not feel alright it would not be good to stay here I *need* fresh air'.

So Simhi and Shynah went back from the path they had came from, it was easy for them to track where they were because of the torches when they finally did went back to the same place where there were different tunnels Simhi gave a sigh, 'This is our only chance this *must* be the exit from here'.

Saying thus they all went in that opening while they were walking they heard footsteps it surprised them then they realized it must be MS Madelline who must have came here to give them there food.

Simhi didn' know what to do she somehow managed to blend with the rocks with her shirt but Shynah was in trouble she couldn't hide anywhere so Simhi thought of a plan while MS Madelline was coming closer and closer Simhi somehow managed to escape from her sight but to save Shynah she took a pebble and threw it MS Madelline who became distracted went there without noticing Shynah.

'Hurry we don't have much time' said Simhi, they rushed towards the ending of the door where they saw a little ray of light as they got closer Simhi found out there was a trap door but it was locked.

Simhi then remembered the library keys which she had in her pocket with a hope of luck Simhi took it out from her pocket and tried to open the trap door and it opened!

When they both finally came out from the trap door they realized it was the same trap door in which MS Madelline had came that day. With a sigh of relief they both hurried towards the dormitory but to there surprise someone held them bith and tugged them hard it was MS. Madelline!

'Where do you think you are going ?' asked MS. Madelline then she quietly tied Simhi and Shynah up and threw them roughly towards the bush, 'I would do something about you both tomorrow but today I am exhausted plus it is almost night no body would be hear right now and you two should also get to know who you both are dealing with this is both of your punishment so stay here in the harsh weather at least you would then know never to underestimate *me*' said MS Madelline coldly.

9

Finally An Escape!

Simhi cried for help she couldn't even move it was night time nobody was there Simhi was exhausted and also had many bruises on her but still she didn't give up and tried her best to be spotted by someone or be heord by someone.

Many hours passed by nobody came in there orea Simhi waited and waited nobody came she became frustrated Shynah began to cry her health was getting really worse she didn't have the energy to even talk.

'My health I am ill Simhi I might faint my head feels heavy' said Shynah meekly Simhi was alormed by Shynah's health getting worse. 'She *ought* to be in bed right now because of me Shynah is so ill' thought Simhi, she bit her lips while thinking this.

Simhi pulled out a few blades of grass out from the wet soil and collected enough to make a small patch, 'Shynah lie down here I hope there is no insects in the grass' said Simhi to Shynah. Shynah at first resisted but too tired out that she was she soon agreed and lay down.

But nature wasn't too easy on them soon it storted to rain Simhi and Shynah couldn't do much as they couldn't walk Simhi tried to cover Shynah by holding a few blades of grass above her to make it as an umbrella but it was of no use. 'Shynah could get severally ill if the rain doesn't stop' thought Simhi.

She held the blade of grass above Shynah though it was not really effective and Simhi also cried for help she wasn't feeling very well herself because of what she felt it hord to scream very loudly.

As soon as it felt all hope was lost Simhi suddenly remembered about Nand.He comes everyday from tuition at this time so he might be coming, thought Simhi herself didn't know what time it was She thought what to do with Shynah, 'Should I leave her here and go and try to find Nand or should I stay heor and protect Shynah' after much thinking Simhi couldn't think of a solution.

'Simhi you go and find Nand don't think about me' said Shynah in a trembling voice and what was this Achuu ACHUUUU Shynah had gotten a cold! Simhi was horrified but still acted as calm as possible so that Shynah doesn't get too panicked.

So at the end Simhi very difficultly waddled oround to find Nand.

Her luck was with her because she saw a Mc Lorren coming back! Simhi smiled and was relieved because it was the cor of Nand's uncle she saw Nand coming out of the cor 'Nand! Nand!' look I am here *Nand!!!!*'.

Thankfully Uncle Rodger heord her scream, 'Nand some child is calling out your name what is going on?'. Nand was also surprised to heor a girl scream he had became lonely after Simhi and Shynah went away.

When Uncle Rodger and Nand ran to locate the sound they saw Simhi tied up. 'What in the world' exclaimed Uncle Rodger. Simhi cried out, 'Uncle you didn't believe what I said, MS Madelline was the one who did this to us there is

Shynah too behind'.

Nand immediately rushed to help but Uncle Rodger thought of something else. Uncle Rodger pulled out his phone and storted taking pictures of Simhi and Shynah who were waddling behind.

'What ore you doing uncle' asked Simhi.

'Oh I was just clicking photos to give as proof to the police about all the events that took place' said Uncle Rodger who winked while saying this, Simhi winked back.

'Uncle Rodger *is* clever' thought Simhi proud of having to know such a clever person.

Uncle Rodger was horrified to see Shynah's condition, Shynah looked so weak that she couldn't even taking properly, both Uncle Rodger and Nand didn't mind the pouring rain.

Nand thought quick and gave his Mackintosh that he was weoring to Shynah to weor, Shynah felt better instantly after weoring the Mackintosh.

Soon Simhi and Shynah were rushed to the hospital for their checkup where as Uncle Rodger went inside the orphanage, all the children were surprised to see a big man being drenched in rain coming frantically in the dinning table where the children were doing their dinner and calling out urgently MS Madelline's name.

Uncle found MS Madelline in her office humming a song to herself and drinking her tea, Ms Madelline was surprised to see Uncle Rodger fully drenched coming towords her like a hurricane, 'What happen to you Mr Rodger you look like you were out in the rain' asked MS Madelline trying to hide her astonishment

Uncle Rodger came straight to the point and accused MS. Madelline. Uncle Rodger forcefully brought MS. Madelline in front of the police.

Just imagine the surprise of MS. Madelline after she heors the story of Simhi's and Shynah's breakthrough!

10

The Truth

A day passed all the children in the orphanage also got to know about Simhi and Shynah's adventures all the children were horrified after listening to their story.

Simhi was recovering well she was allowed to go back home, in her orphanage, but Shynah's in her case her health was getting worse and worse she had to stay in the hospital for a couple of days.

When Simhi arrived in the orphanage there was a huge crowd, everyone wanted to know about the story of her and Shynah, even the grownups were eagerly waiting to know about the news just like the children.

When Simhi was narrating the story to the keen listeners Uncle Rodger came in the orphanage and in the room where Simhi was telling her tale, 'Simhi I want to tell you something' he exclaimed but before he could say anything else the children shushed him up, 'Can't you see Simhi is narrating her story'.

Uncle Rodger gave a chuckle and step back and went out of the room and waited for Simhi to finnish narrating her story, 'Before children used to treat me like a specialty but now look at them' he thought witha grinn on his face, he waited till Simhi had finished narrating her story.

'Yes Uncle Rodger why were you calling me that time?' asked Simhi.

'Look Simhi' continued Uncle Rodger, 'Please listen carefully I have found a very important piece of information, 'Then why are you telling me?' asked Simhi dumbstruck.

'You would understand it after you get to know' continued Uncle Rodger, 'Simhi look your parents hadn't died due to any accident or anything but MS. Madellineeee was the one who killed your mother, she was the sister of your mother'.

Simhi frozed she was shocked, 'How is this possible do you have any proof about it' asked Simhi. 'Yes obviously I would have an evidence while we were interrogating MS. Madellineeee and searching her office documents there it could be seen that it is registered that her and your mother is the same person when we showed this to MS. Madellineeee in a fury she told everything' saying thus Uncle Rodger took out his phone and in high volume turned on a recording of MS. Madellineeee.

> "*Fine this is true I DID try to trap Simhi in the dungeons so that I could kill her I did not want to target Shynah but she too was entering in this fight so that day I knocked her out so that I can get rid of her I did kill MY sister and brother in law because I was jalouse of them both living in such a rich life I wanted to kill Simhi too but that time I underestimated her and thought that what would she possibly do but I was wrong EXTREMELY wrong.*"

'See!' exclaimed Uncle Rodger, 'The clothes of a man, a women are none other then the clothes of your mother and father and that dresses of a small two year old girl was none other than your dresses and that pendulum you were talking about has a family image which is your family and the word lioness is inscripted on it because your name's meaning *is* a lioness here you go' Uncle Rodger then gave the pendulum to the dazed Simhi, 'I had asked the police to give the pendulum back and they agreed your parents have done a right job naming you Simhi the little lioness' said Uncle Rodger.

Simhi quickly wore the pendulum around her neck she then kept and kept looking at her parents for a long time with her teary eyes, Uncle Rodger left Simhi with a smile.

Simhi then suddenly remembered of MS Anny, 'Uncle Rodger where is MS Anny' asked Simhi just then MS. Anny came from nowhere and hugged Simhi.

Simhi was surprised when she saw MS Anny but she was too glad to see her that she didn't ask her anything.

Later that day while everyone were sitting in the dinning hall eating lunch MS Anny finally disclosed to Simhi and all the other girls that she had quit her job because she knew Simhi and Shynah were in danger ans she couldn't rescue them if she had her job, she had heared MS Madelline talking about a sort of dungeon and a trap door then MS Anny saw the map in MS. Madellineeee's office during the day she had went to quit her job then she realized that it was actually a map of the dungeons and also that she had left Simhi and Shynah in the dungeons that day in between because she heard the footsteps of MS Madelline coming.

Everyone listened and applauded MS Anny.

'You are like a spy mom' said Simhi realy impressed by Ms Anny's quick thinking.

'But MS Anny were you here the whole time or something because when I asked about you you just came from nowhere.' asked Simhi.

'Well yes I had came to the dungeon's trap door in the orphanage because I was worried about you but when I saw you and MS. Madelline together then I hid behind the bush and then saw the whole affairs then I sneaked out of that place and came back the next day in the early morning when I again I hid behind the bush to see what was happening when I saw you and you know the rest of the story ' said MS Anny with a smile.

'Where did this dungeon even lead to-' asked Simhi but was interrupted by Uncle Rodger, he was also standing amongst the crowd, 'Oh I forgot to tell you the dungeons was actually underneath a bungalow and it is connected with the orphanage and the bungalow is your parents *house!'*

It shocked Simhi. Her parents house, HER parents house!.

11

Home At Last

The next day Simhi and Nand were waiting outside the orphanage, as it was Sunday Nand didn't had school, they were waiting for Uncle Rodger who had gone to pick up Shynah from the hospital.

'I say' continued Nand 'Fancy having to go to such aa adventure if I were you I would have escaped from their prety quickly because of my bravery and intelligence.'

'Oh, stop bragging said Simhi, 'When I had thrown a pebble at MS Madelline that day in the office you got so scared that you ran away.'

Nand went red with embarresment, but luckily for him Simhi needn't to tease him more as they heard a honk just then.

It was the honk of a Mc Larren which came zooming in and stopped right infront of Simhi and Nand, Simhi had never seen the Mc Larren up from this close it was realy beautifull the lifting doors, the interior it was all really mesmerizing

Simhi couldn't believe that she hadn't ever noticed the Mc Laren car ever before.

The interior of Mc Laren is carbon black in clor and the sterring wheel has a very good grip inside of it, it was all well mantained

Uncle Rodger came out from inside with Shynah following by, Simhi and Nand quickly rushed towards Shynah, Simhi hugged her.

'Thank god you are fine but you *ought* to be yesterday because it was so fun telling everyone about our stories, the way Uncle Rodger came out of the dormitory like a thunderstorm dragging MS Madelline but no issues you can hear yesterday's story later' said Simhi all in under a breath.

Shynah was fully recovered she had a very large bandage oer her head which had to be wrapped around the wound for some time. Shynah still had a little bit of cold but it was going to get cured after a few days.

'Let's go inside and tell everyone else that you have come back from the hospitall jolly everyone thought you are a hero Shynah and you were so brave yesterday you *are* brave' said Simhi. Nand did not like the way the conversation was going on so he interrupted them, 'Let's go inside.'

But before the trio went inside they heard Uncle Rodger yelling, 'Wait! I have a small thing to talk to you about.' Simhi as wella as the other two were surprised. What *does* Uncle Rodger want to talk about for?'

Uncle Rodger seemed to be very excited by his 'news' that he was going to share to the others his eyes beemed.

'I have decided that I am adopting Nand and making him the future heir of my business as I think hje is capable of doing so' but before the other two could react Uncle Rodger also added, 'And also I am going to take you both home with me if you like too,but I have a condition that if you will come you all will also have to go to the school with

Nand and I will be giving you both good education'

Uncle Rodger thought Simhi and Shynah would have been thoroughly happy but Simhi wasn't.

'What's the matter Simhi what's wrong?' asked Uncle Rodger who was very surprised of Simhi not being excited.

'Well I would go in one condition' begain Simhi slowly, 'If you also take Ms Anny with you then I will be happy to go because she had quit her job because of us and she is soon going to run out of money then how would she pay rent?'.

Simhi said this, she didnn't know what Uncle Rodger was going tho say.

Uncle Rodger was in awe with Simhi's kindness so he agreed but Ms Anny also set a condition, 'I would go and live there but I would still like to work here too this has after all been my memorable job so how could I leave it?'.

Uncle Rodger agreed with Ms Anny's conditions and then picked everyone up and took them to there new homes where they could finally live happily and for Ms Madelline she was living un - happily in her prison sell.

Acknowledgements

It was always my dream that I write a book and today I am writing one. I am always interested in writing mystical type of stories, this is my first book will it be my last? No, I would wright way more books maybe I even make a sequence of it.

I would like to thank Notion Press for giving me an opportunity to write this book also I would like to thank the readers who are reading this book you have supported me to wright this book. I would also like to thank Sudha Murty too, to give me an inspiration for wrighting this book, If you are reading this book then this would be my dream to meet you.